Once Upon a... Fairytale

Natalia and Lauren O'Hara

Dear Reader,

Have you ever dreamed of casting a spell, feasting with fairies or riding home on a unicorn?

Here, in this magical world, you can.

Around every corner there is a new adventure. You can do, and see, and be whatever you wish!

The hero of this tale is *you*.

Once upon . . .

a golden morning

a fairy's birthday

a cosy teatime

a rainy Tuesday

a broken armchair

in a land ruled by a wise, kind Queen, there was . . .

a well-dressed puss

a jolly woodcutter's son

a gentle knight

a clever princess

a mighty witch

a courteous fox

a kindly farm girl

a friendly
gingerbread man

who lived in . . .

a pretty cottage
by a river.

a tree in a playground.

a tower on a
windy hill.

a creepy, crumbly
haunted shack.

a shoe on the village
high street.

And one fine day, at the door there
came a knock . . . knock . . . KNOCK!

It was a messenger from the Queen.

"I come with horrid news,"
he said. "A villain has cursed
our land and turned . . .

all the babies into pigs.

the mums and
dads into rocks.

the Queen and court
to birds and bugs.

our dinners into socks.

"The Queen sent me to find a hero – to fight the villain and break the curse. I've asked in every corner, but no one will go.

Will *you* be our hero?"

"I will!" said the hero, and took a cloak as red as a berry, and went out into the world.

Soon the hero came to a river, and heard
a watery "Help!"

A merman was trapped in a net. The hero
cut the net open, and out he leapt.

"You saved me, friend," he cried.
"In thanks, I will give you . . .

a vanishing cloak."

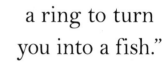

a ring to turn
you into a fish."

a pair of magic shoes."

a berry to make you shrink."

a magical flying broom."

"Thank you," said the hero, and walked on.

Before long the hero came to a garden. In a space between the flowers, some very unusual people were having a feast.

"Join us," they cried.
"Thank you," said the hero, and sat down to eat . . .

newt pie and pig-tail pudding, with warlocks.

partridge stew and toasted chestnuts, with forest folk.

gold bars and ruby sprinkles, with gnomes.

roasted stars, mashed snow cloud and
fresh-buttered sunbeams, with fairies.

Then the hero came to a mountain, and heard
a growly "Help!"

A bear king was caught in a trap. The hero
snapped the rope, and out he leapt.

"You saved me, friend," he roared.
"In thanks, I will give you . . .

a sword that
fights by itself."

a magic wand."

a hole to vanish
things in."

a bow and arrow
that never miss."

a potion to make
nasty things nice."

"Thank you," said the hero, and – too
excited to look – fell off the mountain.

Down the hero fell – and down.

But a kindly moth was flying past, and she caught the hero on her back.

She drifted over the patchwork land . . .

. . . and dropped the hero down in a meadow.

The hero came to a bush, and heard a tinkly "Help!"

A pixie was stuck in a spider's web. The hero
broke the web open, and out she leapt.

"You saved me, friend," she squeaked.
"In thanks, I will give you . . .

a shimmery unicorn

a blue whale

a flying bed

a talking wolf

to come when you call."
"Thank you," said the hero, and walked on.

At last the hero came to a deep, dark wood. No bees buzzed.
No children played. No birds sang.

Through the trees, a dim light winked.
Creeping closer, the hero saw . . .

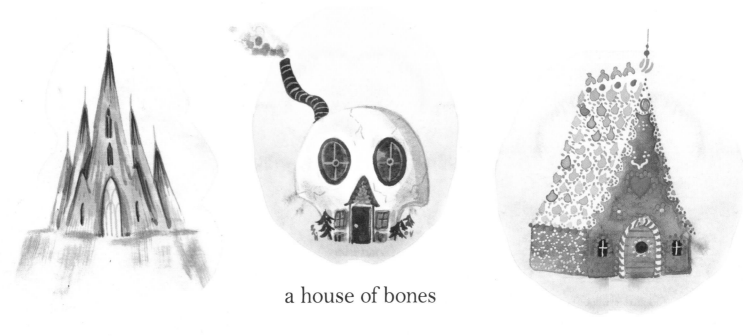

a house of bones

a palace of ice

a gingerbread cottage

a sinister cabin   a dark and twisted castle

with guards on every side.

So the hero took out . . .

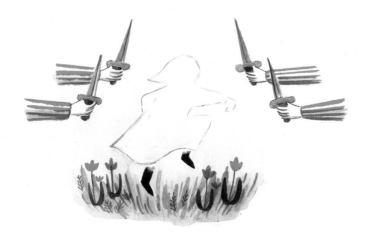

the cloak, and skipped
past the guards.

the ring, and swam
up the drainpipe.

the shoes, and wished
to be inside.

the berry, and ran
under the door.

the broom, and flew
to the window.

The hero was in a room filled with horrible things.
High on a shelf was a box that said 'Curses'.

From behind, there came a low creak.

The hero spun round and saw the villain –

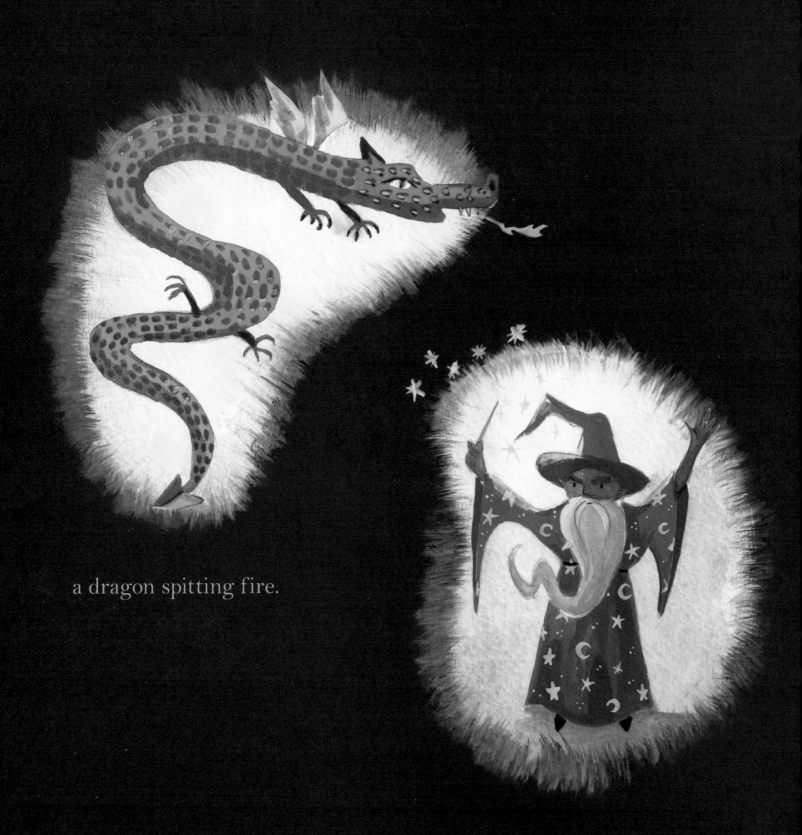

a dragon spitting fire.

a wizard with a wand.

a demon with spiky horns.

an ogre with a club.

a hypnotic dancing goblin.

Trembling, the hero grabbed . . .

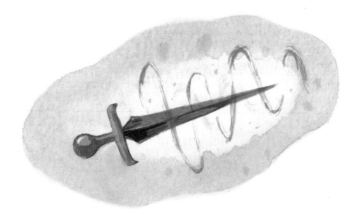

the magic sword, and
fought the villain.

the wand, and turned the
villain into a mouse.

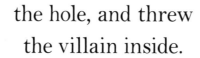

the hole, and threw
the villain inside.

the bow and arrow, and the
villain ran away squealing.

the potion, and made the villain
into a nice little baby.

The box of curses went *puff* and was gone.

"Hooray!" shouted the hero, and skipped outside.

But all the guards came chasing after. Closer they came – and closer.
The hero reached a cliff – and there was nowhere left to run.

"Help!" yelped the hero – and just then saw . . .

the unicorn, and flew away
in a cloud of stardust.

the blue whale, and
leapt on her back.

the flying bed, and snuggled
all the way home.

the talking wolf, and rode
over hills and forests.

When the hero got back, the curse was broken. There was a marvellous party and everyone came.

"Hero," said the Queen, "you have saved us all.
In thanks, I will give you . . .

a flying ship."

a magical feast that
never ends."

a castle with
golden towers."

a faraway desert island."

a brimming, glittering
treasure trove."

"Thank you," said the hero, and everyone cheered.

Then they yawned. It was late, you see.
So they all went home to bed. Except the hero,
who put on a cloak as red as a berry, and went . . .

. . . to find a new adventure.

Magic

Adventure

Fish Pond

For Astrea, who is a hero.

First published 2022 by Macmillan Children's Books
an imprint of Pan Macmillan
The Smithson, 6 Briset Street, London EC1M 5NR
EU representative: Macmillan Publishers Ireland Limited,
1st Floor, The Liffey Trust Centre, 117-126 Sheriff Street Upper,
Dublin 1, D01 YC43
Associated companies throughout the world
www.panmacmillan.com

Hardback ISBN: 9781529045772
Paperback ISBN: 9781529045789

MIX
Paper | Supporting
responsible forestry
FSC® C116313